The Feather

DISCARD

D1044469

For Morgan,
with love
— F. P.

To my dear
nephew Ambroise
— S. F.

Barefoot Books
2067 Massachusetts Ave
Cambridge, MA 02140

Series Editor: Gina Nuttall
Text copyright © 2011 by Fran Parnell
Illustrations copyright © 2003 & 2011 by Sophie Fatus
The moral rights of Fran Parnell and Sophie Fatus have been asserted

Graphic design by Helen Chapman, West Yorkshire, UK
Reproduction by B&P International, Hong Kong
Printed in China on 100% acid-free paper by Printplus, Ltd
This book was typeset in Chalkduster, Gilligan's Island and Sassoon Primary
The illustrations were prepared in acrylics

Sources:
Calvino, Italo. *Italian Folktales*. George Martin, Translator.
Harcourt, Brace, Jovanovich, Inc., New York, 1980.

Chopra, Jagmohan. *Folk Tales of Italy*.
Sterling Publishers Pvt, 1985.

ISBN 978-1-84686-562-6

Library of Congress Cataloging-in-Publication Data is
available under LCCN 2011002937

1 3 5 7 9 8 6 4 2

The Feathered Ogre

A Story from Italy

Retold by Fran Parnell · Illustrated by Sophie Fatus

Barefoot Books
Step inside a story

Contents

CHAPTER 1 – page 6

AN IMPOSSIBLE TASK

CHAPTER 2 – page 13

A FRIGHTENING JOURNEY

CHAPTER 3 – page 23

A Helping Hand

CHAPTER 4 – page 29

The Ogre's Secret

CHAPTER 5 – page 38

The Great Escape

AN
IMPOSSibLe TaSK

Long ago in a country far away,
the king was very sick. The royal doctor
came to his bedside. First, he made the
king say, "Ahhh."

Then, he counted the beats of the
king's heart. Finally, he shook his head.
"Only a magic feather from the
Ogre's back can cure you, Your Royal
Highness," he said. All the noble knights
and ladies gasped. They were horrified.

The Feathered Ogre lived on an island far to the north. Everyone in the kingdom was afraid of him.

Every year he jumped into a boat and came to the mainland. He captured one hundred of the most tasty and tender young men and women.

He took them back to his island and
stored them for food. One year he even
snatched the king's older daughter. She
had been visiting her aunt in the north.

Many brave men had tried to stop
the Ogre. Many set off to the Ogre's den,
but none had ever returned.

The very sick king sighed. It was a huge sigh. Then he announced, "I will give a reward to whoever brings me a feather from the Ogre's back.

"I will give him my beautiful younger daughter in marriage. I will also give him half of my kingdom."

I don't want to marry!

But in his heart, the king was sad. He did not believe it could be done. And, in their hearts, his people agreed with him. The journey was so frightening. It was utterly impossible to pluck a feather right from the evil Ogre's back.

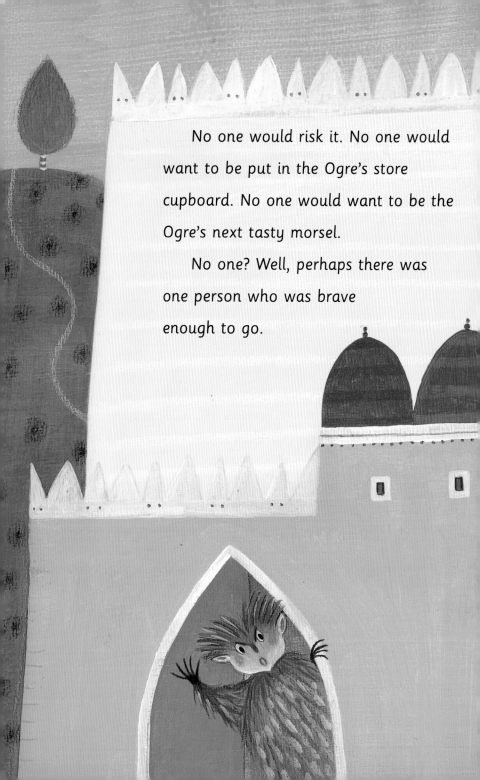

No one would risk it. No one would want to be put in the Ogre's store cupboard. No one would want to be the Ogre's next tasty morsel.

No one? Well, perhaps there was one person who was brave enough to go.

CHAPTER 2

A Frightening Journey

Pírolo was one of the king's gardeners. He was the youngest one. But he was tired of weeding the royal potato patch. He was fed up with picking fat caterpillars off the royal cabbages.

When he heard about the reward, his eyes became dreamy. He longed for a wild adventure. He imagined half a kingdom of his own.

The only bad part was marrying the younger princess. She always made faces at him from the palace windows.

However, Pírolo decided to try and
get the feather. He threw down his
spade and found a strong walking stick.
Then he set off to the far north.

Pírolo traveled for many days. He went uphill and he went downhill. He walked through valleys where the grass was as soft as silk and as green as a frog. He walked over rocky cliffs where the rough stones were as lumpy and twisted as a witch's nose.

Finally, he reached the shore at the end of the kingdom. In front of him was the sea.

And across the sea was the Feathered Ogre's island. Pírolo stood there and wondered how he might get across.

Suddenly he heard the splash
of oars and a person sighing. The
sighs were long and sad.

I am so tired!

A rickety wooden boat was
drifting toward him over the waves.
In the boat sat the oldest man that
Pírolo had ever seen.

His face was as wrinkled as a raisin. He had a long white beard. The tip of it trailed over the side of the boat into the salty water. The boat reached the shore.

Hello, old man!

"Good day!" called Pírolo in a cheery voice. "Will you row me over to the Feathered Ogre's island?"

Hop in and I will row you across!

The boatman looked at Pírolo with
tired eyes. Then he spoke to Pírolo
with a very tired voice. Pírolo thought
it was the weariest sound in the world.

"Traveler, I have rowed from shore
to shore for a thousand years. I am
worn out to my bones. The Feathered
Ogre has put a spell on me and I
cannot get out of this boat. So, sir,
it does not matter to me if there is a
passenger in it or not."

Pírolo shook his head sadly at the
boatman's gloomy tale. Then he jumped
into the little boat.

CHAPTER 3

A Helping Hand

When they reached the island, the boatman pointed to a huge wooden door. It was set into the cliff nearby. Pírolo took a deep breath. He knew what he had to do. He marched bravely across the sand and banged on the door with his walking stick.

After a while, the door slowly creaked open. Pírolo raised his stick again. He was ready to give the Ogre a bop on the nose. But it wasn't the ugly Ogre standing behind the door.

Instead, it was a beautiful girl. She had bright blue eyes. She looked at Pírolo with a puzzled frown. "You're not the Feathered Ogre!" she said. "Who are you? Why are you here?"

Hello, I am a princess!

Pírolo explained everything to the girl. She was surprised. "Why, the king is my father!" she said. "That wicked old Ogre captured me last year when I was visiting my auntie. He didn't eat me because I offered to keep his cave spick and span for him.

"I helped the other people escape from him. I fed the Ogre mutton instead. Now I want to go home too.

"If you help me to find the
way, I will get a feather for you."
Of course, Pírolo agreed.

I'll help you

"Come into the cave and hide under the table," said the princess. "The Ogre will be back soon!"

Pírolo dived under the table just as the door flew open. The Feathered Ogre burst in.

CHAPTER 4

The Ogre's Secret

The Ogre looked horrible. He was scowling. His face was as scrunched as a rotten cabbage. "Where is my supper?" he shouted.

"Here it is, Ogre dear," said the princess. "You munched the last man yesterday. So I have made delicious dumplings for you tonight."

"Bah!" roared the Ogre. And he stuffed all of the dumplings into his mouth at once. "Tomorrow I will catch more tasty human beings for my supper." Then the Feathered Ogre wiped his chin on one feathery arm.

Why are you laughing, Ogre?

"Hah, hah, hah!" he sniggered.
"Every time I sit in the boat with that
old boatman, I laugh to myself. If only
he knew!" And he wiped a tear of
laughter from his eye.

"If only he knew what, Ogre dear?"
asked the princess.

31

Oh, no!

"If only he knew how easy it is for him to escape from my magic! He could be as free as the air. All he has to do is give his passenger the oars to hold and then jump quickly out of the boat. The passenger would be stuck in his place instead.

"The passenger would be the
one rowing from shore to shore until
doomsday. Hah, hah, hah!"

Pírolo was listening carefully under
the table.

"Ogre dear, you look tired,"
murmured the princess thoughtfully.
"Why don't you have a little nap?"

"Mmmm," said the Feathered Ogre
with a big yawn. "That is a good idea.
I am tired out." And he put his head
down on the table.

The girl stroked the Ogre's feathers and sang to him. Finally, he fell into a deep sleep and began to snore.

Now my father will get better!

The princess quickly pulled a magic feather from his back. She threw it under the table to Pírolo.

"Ow!" howled the Ogre, waking up.

"I've been stung!"

"There, there, Ogre dear," the princess said softly. "It was just a little spark from the fire that burned one of your pretty feathers. Go back to sleep."

"Hmmm," said the Ogre sleepily. He put his head back on the table. Soon he was snoring again.

"Quick!" whispered the princess to Pírolo. "Now is our chance. RUN!"

CHAPTER 5

The Great Escape

Let's get out of here!

Pírolo and the princess held
hands and ran across the cave. They
opened the huge door and rushed
outside into the daylight. But the
door slammed shut with a loud bang.

Come back here!

As Pírolo and the princess ran toward the boat, they heard the Ogre wake up. "Aaaargh!" the Ogre raged angrily.

"Row, boatman, row!" cried Pírolo as they flung themselves into the boat. Behind them, the door of the cave burst open and the Ogre charged out.

"Come back!" shouted the Ogre. He hopped up and down in the sand.

But the boatman rowed as if the sea was on fire. At the other side, Pírolo and the princess jumped out safely.

We will be home soon.

Then they told the boatman
how to escape from the spell. The
boatman smiled for the first time
in a thousand years!

Pírolo and the princess ran toward home. The princess clutched the precious feather in her hand. Uphill and downhill they dashed. Finally, they reached the palace.

I am well again!

The magic feather cured the king instantly. He was delighted to see his older daughter again. He even danced a jig around the throne room.

He kept his promise and gave Pírolo half of his kingdom. And he let Pírolo marry the older daughter instead of the younger one.

Everyone was happy!

We are getting married!

Everyone? Well, everyone except for the wicked Feathered Ogre. While Pírolo and the princess were running home, the boatman rowed back to the island.

They won't get away with it!

When he got there, the Ogre leaped into the boat with a roar. "I will catch that nasty pair, you will see," he shouted. "Row faster!"

The Ogre was very angry. So he
did not notice the boatman smile.
The boatman said, "Why don't you
take the oars? A mighty ogre like you
could row much faster than an old
man like me."

The Ogre did not realize that the boatman knew the secret. The Ogre grabbed the oars and sent the boat skimming over the waves like a bird.

But before he could get out at the other side, the boatman jumped out of the boat into the shallow water.

"Hah, hah, hah!" the
boatman laughed. He clicked his
heels in the air with delight.

"I'm free! I'm as free as the
air!" And he ran away over the
pebbly beach.

The Feathered Ogre howled in horror.
Pírolo and the princess heard it far away
in the palace. Now the Ogre was cursed
by his own spell. He had to row the boat
from shore to shore until doomsday.
And, as far as I know, he is still rowing!